S0-CFT-144

Our Tree Named
STEVE

Alan Zweibel

Illustrated by

David Catrow

SCHOLASTIC INC.
New York Toronto London Auckland
Sydney Mexico City New Delhi Hong Kong

Dear Kids,

A long time ago, when you were little, Mom and I took you to where we wanted to build a house for us to live in.

But in order to build there, men had to come and clear the land.

I remember there was one tree, however, that the three of you couldn't stop staring at. Adam thought it was crying, Lindsay said it looked nervous, and Sari, who was only two years old, couldn't pronounce the word *tree*, and called it "Steve."

"I love you, Steve," she kept saying. And then Adam and Lindsay started saying it. And before too long, Mom and I got the hint and asked the builder to please save Steve.

The day we moved in, Steve was there to greet us.

He quickly worked his way into your lives as a swing holder,

target, third base, hiding place, jump-rope turner . . .

. . . and whenever our dryer broke down,

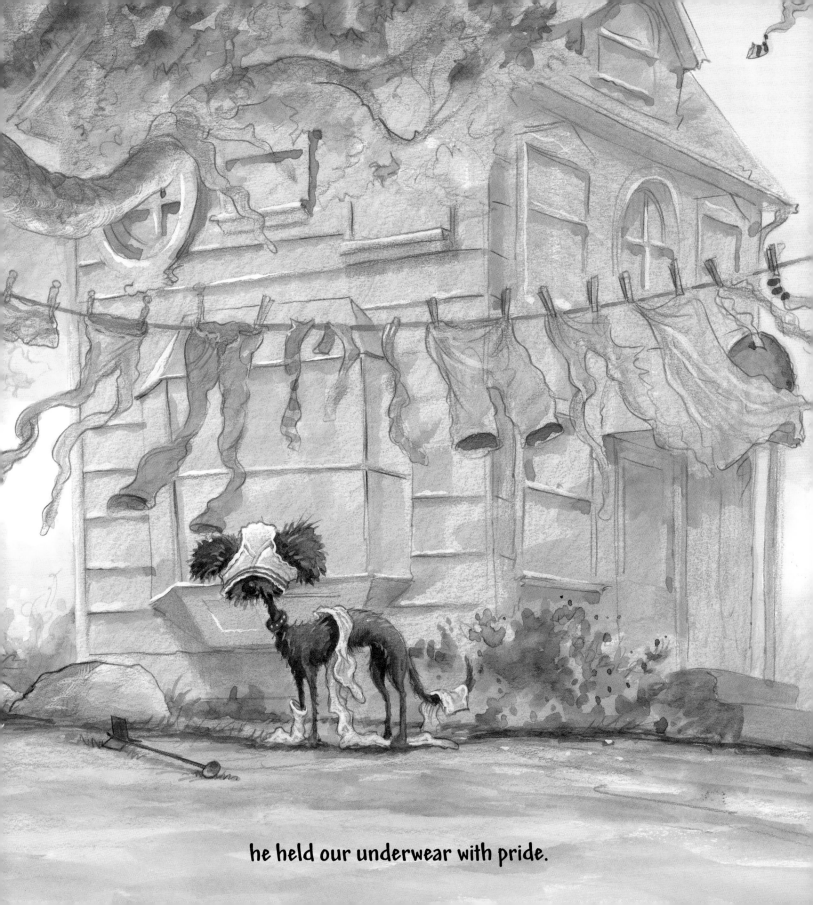

he held our underwear with pride.

Yes, right there in the center of our yard, this weird-looking tree grew to become the center of our outdoor life.

Through all our barbecues, campouts, dance parties . . .

. . . or when Adam and Lindsay started getting crushes on the
Simon kids next door, Steve adjusted to our every need.

And it wasn't always easy. Standing tall through snowstorms
in the winter . . .

. . . or when Uncle Chester napped in the hammock couldn't possibly have been fun.

Not to mention the time that the sewer overflowed and Steve sucked up all the smelly water before it drowned Kirby . . .

. . . then got so sick himself that the tree doctor had to give Steve
a haircut that made him look like a big thumb.

Through the years Mom and I have tried to show you, in a world filled with strangers, the peace that comes with having things you can count on and a safe place to return to after a hard day or a long trip.

Which brings me to the point of this letter. Last week, a storm hit our area . . .

. . . and though we spared Steve's life a long time ago,

this time we couldn't save him.

Are we sad? Sure we are. But even in his final moments, when
he could have fallen on our house, Sari's swings, Kirby's house,

or Mom's garden, Steve performed his last trick and protected
all of us to the very end, and friends like this are hard to find.

So, when you come home from Grandma's next week, Steve will not be able to greet you as he's done in the past. I'm sorry.

But please know that Steve will always be with us.
In our hearts, in our thoughts . . .

. . . and in a different tree at the
other end of our yard.
See you next week.
Love,
Dad

To Robin, Adam, Lindsay, Sari, and Kirby
—A. Z.

To Deborah, for standing by me through all our storms
—D. C.

No part of this publication may be reproduced, stored in a retrieval system, or transmitted in any form or by any means, electronic, mechanical, photocopying, recording, or otherwise, without written permission of the publisher. For information regarding permission, write to G. P. Putnam's Sons, a division of Penguin Young Readers Group, a member of Penguin Group (USA) Inc., 345 Hudson Street, New York, NY 10014.

ISBN 978-0-545-24831-0

Text copyright © 2005 by Alan Zweibel. Illustrations copyright © 2005 by David Catrow. All rights reserved. Published by Scholastic Inc., 557 Broadway, New York, NY 10012, by arrangement with G. P. Putnam's Sons, a division of Penguin Young Readers Group, a member of Penguin Group (USA) Inc. SCHOLASTIC and associated logos are trademarks and/or registered trademarks of Scholastic Inc.

12 11 10 9 8 7 6 5 4 3 2 1   10 11 12 13 14 15/0

Printed in the U.S.A.   08

This edition first printing, January 2010

Designed by Gina DiMassi
Text set in Andy Bold
The art was done in pencil and watercolor.